All scripture quotations, unless otherwise indicated, are taken from the HOLY BIBLE, NEW INTERNATIONAL READER'S VERSION ®.
Copyright © 1995, 1996, 1998 by International Bible Society. All rights reserved.

Published by Big Idea Entertainment, 320 Billingsly Court, Suite 30, Franklin, TN 37067

ISBN: 9781605872612

Printed in China

First Big Idea Printing, April 2011

THE Case OF THE LOST TEMPER

A Lesson in Self-Control

by Doug Peterson

Illustrated by John Trent
and Greg Hardin

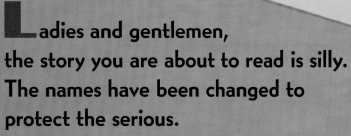

Ladies and gentlemen, the story you are about to read is silly. The names have been changed to protect the serious.

It was a crazy day at police headquarters. Bob the Tomato was jittery and a little bit angry. Maybe he was mad because the Masked Door Slammer was on the loose in the city. Or maybe it was because I had accidentally stapled a burrito to his tie.

Whatever.

It was our job to stop the Masked Door Slammer. My name is Detective Larry the Cucumber, and my partner is Bob. He carries a badge. I carry a badger. Don't ask why.

10:00 a.m. This was it. We got a report of a door slamming in progress! So we leaped into our car and drove straight to 105 Hippity-Hop Lane.

Bob still seemed angry when we rang the doorbell. Maybe he was upset because the bell didn't work. Or maybe it was because he found a taco in his wallet while getting out his badge. I wondered where I had put that taco.

"Hello, ma'am," Bob said. "We had a report that someone has been slamming doors in anger." "Door slamming, you say?" said Mrs. Carrot. "I don't know anything about it."

Mrs. Carrot was hiding something. I could tell.

Her daughter Laura smiled sweetly. I made a note that she could be our Masked Door Slammer.

"We need to keep an eye on this house," I told Bob, as we returned to our car. "I can sense anger. Someone has been losing their temper."

But Bob didn't answer. He was steaming mad about something. Maybe he was still upset about the doorbell.

Or maybe it was because he had just sat down on a plate of nachos, which I had left on the car seat.

10:45 a.m. We decided to "stake-out" the Carrot house. A stakeout is when you keep an eye on a place and wait for something to happen. We were going to wait for the Masked Door Slammer to show up. But first, we went home to put on disguises.

12:00 p.m. Bob and I met on the street corner right across from the Carrot house.
Bob had put on a fake mustache and glasses. But he seemed angrier than ever.

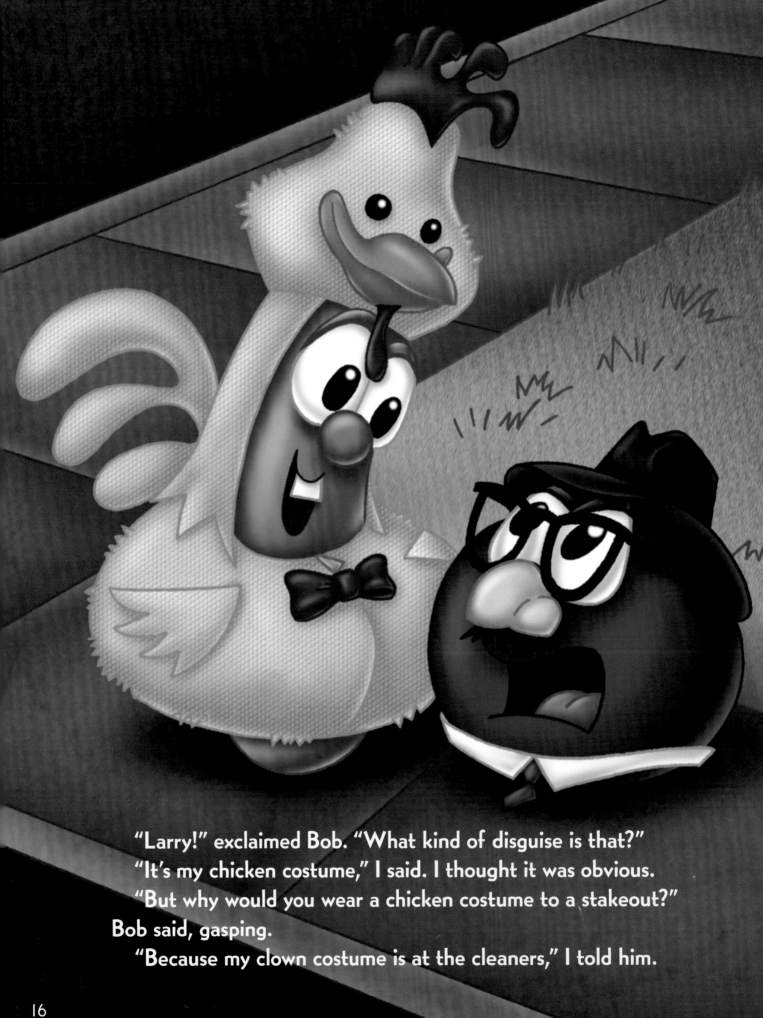

"Larry!" exclaimed Bob. "What kind of disguise is that?"
"It's my chicken costume," I said. I thought it was obvious.
"But why would you wear a chicken costume to a stakeout?"
Bob said, gasping.
"Because my clown costume is at the cleaners," I told him.

"Ahhhhhhh!"

Bob screamed. Then he tried to control himself. "When we're on a stakeout, the idea is for *no one* to notice us. When you wear a chicken costume, *everyone* will notice us! It's crazy!"

He had a point there. Maybe it would be better if I did not wear the chicken costume.

"Oops," I said as I tried to take off the costume. The zipper broke. Bob clunked his head against the light post.

That had to hurt.

12:34 p.m. Still no door slams at the Carrot house. They were playing it cool. I wish I could say the same about Bob.

"Larry! What are you doing?" grumbled Bob.

"I'm playing on my skateboard," I said. I did not understand why Bob couldn't figure these things out himself.

"But why would you play on a skateboard when we're trying to keep an eye on the Carrot house?" Bob asked.

"Because nothing is happening.
I'm bored," I said.

"But don't you think people are going
to notice us when they see a chicken on
a skateboard?" growled Bob.

I thought long and hard about
that one. "You don't think
anyone has ever seen a chicken
skateboarding before?" I asked.

"Noooooo!"
Bob screamed.

1:25 p.m. The pizza delivery guy finally showed up with my food. That was when Bob completely lost his temper. He ran around, wild with anger. Bob yelled, but I was not sure what he was trying to say. It was something about how I should not order pizza on a stakeout. When I asked whether I should eat steak on a stakeout, Bob started shouting even louder.

Suddenly a thought came to me.

"You know, Bob, letting your anger run wild is kind of like letting a crook run wild in the city," I said to him. "Crooks hurt people. And so does anger when it is out of control."

All at once Bob stopped running around.

"When our anger runs wild, we say mean things," I added. "Sometimes, we even slam doors and break things. We hurt others and rob ourselves of happiness."

Bob took a deep breath and counted to 10. "Maybe you're right," he said. "God is slow to anger. I wonder . . ." And that was when it happened.

SLAMMM!

A door slam rang out like a shot. It came from the back of the Carrot house!

Bob and I dashed across the street
and pounded on the front door.
   Laura Carrot was shocked when she
opened the door and we barreled inside.
   "Okay, where is it?" I said.
   "Where's what?" asked Laura.
   "The slamming door!" Bob shouted.

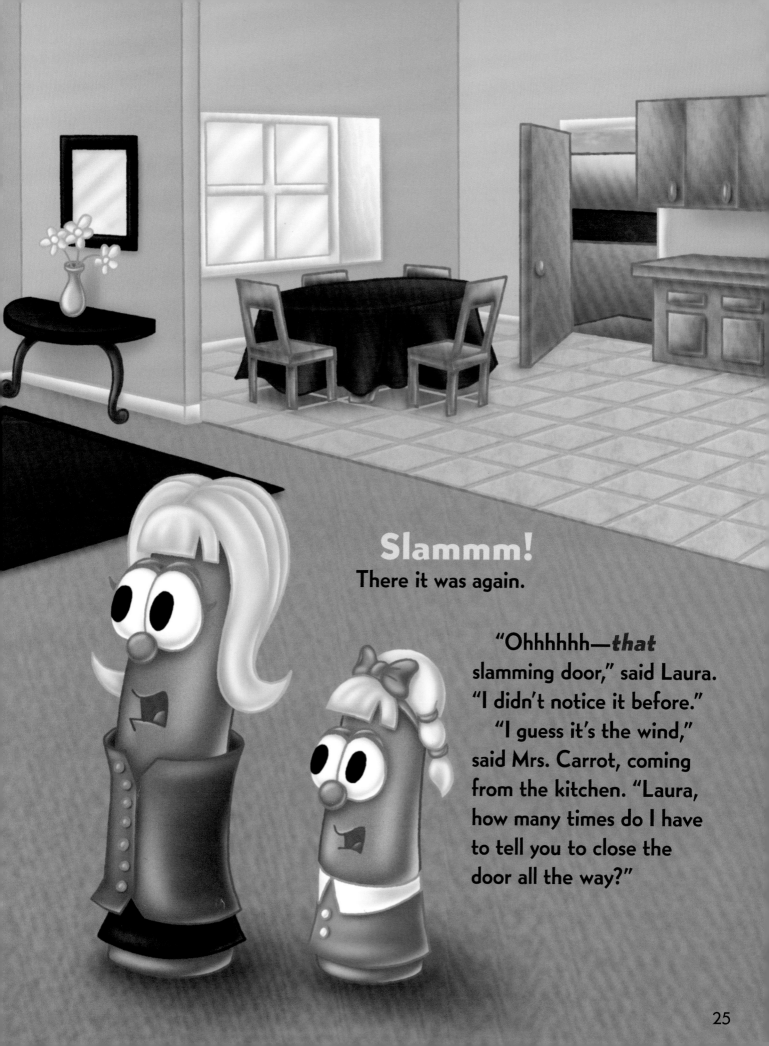

Slammm!
There it was again.

"Ohhhhhh—*that* slamming door," said Laura. "I didn't notice it before."

"I guess it's the wind," said Mrs. Carrot, coming from the kitchen. "Laura, how many times do I have to tell you to close the door all the way?"

Mrs. Carrot was right.
The back door was being slammed
by the wind. There was no Masked Door Slammer after all!
I looked at Bob. Bob looked at me. Then we both burst
out laughing.
Even Laura, Mrs. Carrot, and my badger joined in the laughter.
The case was closed.

2:00 p.m. It was nice to see Bob happy again. For most of the day, anger had robbed him of his joy. But his happiness was back. On the way home, Bob could not stop smiling. After all, it was not every day that he got to see a giant chicken skateboarding down the street and eating pizza.

Now if I can just get this zipper fixed . . .

A foolish person lets
his anger run wild.
But a wise person keeps
himself under control.
Proverbs 29:11